CATTAIL STORIES

CATTAIL STORIES

Graciela Trevisan

Copyright © 2019 Graciela Trevisan
Illustrations by Andrew Ramer
All rights reserved.
ISBN 9781076197870

Cover illustration by Andrew Ramer
Book design by Erin McElroy
Author photograph by Lisa Rofel

To

Lisa, for her love, support and unconditional
help with this book.
Ute, our super adorable cat, who helped me
with this book almost to the end. In her honor.
My mother, in memoriam, who looked
forward to this book coming out.

Contents

Acknowledgments viii
The Woman Who Made A River 1
Antonia 5
Grandma 9
Matilde 14
Paula 19
Aurora 25
Emilia 31
The Two Antonias 35
Carolina 39
Eva 46
Lisa 50
The Time The Town Went Dark 56
Just A Little Scare (Aurora, again) 60
Victoria 63
The Moonlight Orange Tree 69

Cecilia *73*
The Beginning *77*
The End (for now) *86*

Acknowledgments

This book was in the making for many years. The persons who supported me, encouraged me and read all, some or one of these stories are very numerous. I express my gratitude to all of them.

Special thanks to Lisa Rofel, Leslie Kirk Campbell, Nelly Vuksic, Megan Moodie, Steve Ciano, Sharon Hallas and Isabel Yrigoyen.

For a long time, the town had needed water for gardens, crops and wells. It couldn't constantly be borrowing water from other towns. It needed to have its own river. Then she, this woman, who had usually passed unnoticed, said, I can make a river. Nobody expected her to do it but it was worth a try. Besides, everyone else was busy with business and family.

This woman (whose name I never learned), went then outside the town, to the site where the river had to be started. All she took with her was a handkerchief. She knelt down and began to dig a small hole in the ground with her hands. When this was big enough, she started to cry. She cried into the hole, and cried and cried and cried until sunset. I will come back tomorrow, she said, getting up and drying her eyes with her handkerchief. She went back every day and the water started to run from the hole, building a stream that became longer and deeper as the days passed by. Her crying was usually silent, but a few times people in the town worried because it was so loud and deep that they were afraid the water would come into the town and there would be a flood.

Nobody cries anymore! the mayor said one afternoon. Everyone is running, in a hurry... But here we have a woman who stops to cry and when she cries she lends a service to our town... His daughter interrupted him and said, don't you care to know why she is crying? Maybe she is sad. He hadn't thought of

The Woman
Who Made A River

There was once a river. And a woman. The woman had existed long before the river. The river was new and deep. With fresh water and ducks and fish. The woman was an ordinary woman, she had been born and raised (we never learned where or when). The story of the river and the woman began when the town's mayor asked, who can make a river?

that, nobody in the town had either, so out he went to the small hole that was becoming a river and asked her, why do you cry so much? Because I am making a river, she answered. Well, but… are you sad? he insisted. A shadow covered her face. She stopped crying, dried her eyes with her handkerchief and sat on the ground. Somebody, whom I loved, lied to me, she said. The mayor, used to hearing people cry for more concrete and practical reasons, couldn't conceal his surprise and left. A lie, he thought in bed at night, can a lie be as important as a river, as big and deep as a river? A lie, well, I also… and he fell asleep.

In a few months, the work was complete. The town now had its own river and the mayor would never have to borrow water from other towns. This has been the biggest achievement of my mayoral career, he thought satisfied, and all it took was asking who could make a river.

The town celebrated its new river with fireworks and dancing. The mayor, the police chief and the parish priest appeared on the improvised stage: the woman was going to be awarded the town's key. But nobody could find her. She was already gone.

However, from that day on, the town's people were able to cry more often, and when the river ran dry (this almost never happened) another woman would go and replenish it. Then, children and ducks, farmers and frogs would cry of happiness while the fish would hurry to come back.

But where did the woman go? you may ask - I don't know. News came years later that she was living in another country and no longer made rivers.

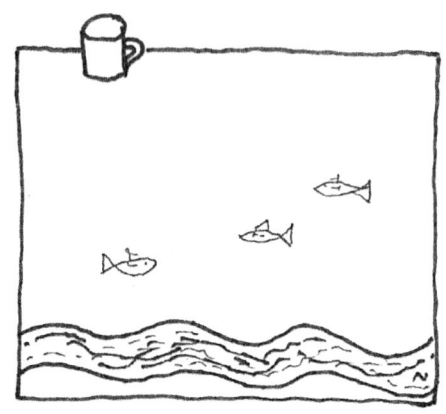

Antonia

There was once an old woman who began to talk with the moon. She spoke so loudly that we woke up and couldn't go back to sleep until the conversation was over. I had heard there were many women who talked with the moon. But this one, Antonia, spoke louder than anyone else. I used to see Antonia passing by with her basket full of bread in the afternoon. I wondered how she could stay up the whole night talking after working hard all morning baking bread in her hut, there, at the edge of town and, then, come and sell it to whoever wanted to buy real homemade bread.

It was one night, in the middle of the autumn, when we first started to hear Antonia. At the beginning nobody knew it was her. Nobody could even identify where the voice was coming from. But when it was a full moon, the conversation was so long and so loud that a lot of people said, that's Antonia talking with the moon! And of the three thousand inhabitants of the town not a single one could understand what they were talking about. One day the parish priest asked her, Antonia, what do you do at night? I sleep, she answered. I mean, the two or three nights right before, during and after the full moon? I talk with my friend, the moon, she said. The parish priest was expecting her to lie, but since she didn't, he sighed and said, go and remember you are only supposed to talk to God.

Nevertheless, Antonia kept talking with the moon. As time passed, we got used to being awake for two or three nights each month. But then people started to sleep during the day. They didn't go to work. Or if they did, they fell asleep behind a counter, behind the cashier, under a car, on a roof, in the middle of the street. Not to mention the school where teachers and we the students could be heard snoring from as far as the church's bell tower where the parish priest had gone to strike the bells and had fallen asleep next to a pigeons' nest. Given the situation, the mayor of the town decided to declare holidays the three days right before, during and after the full moon. Antonia was unaware of what was going on. However, she realized that something was wrong when she came to town and saw that the stores were closed, the church was closed, the school was closed, nobody was on the streets and who is going to buy my bread today!

Nevertheless, Antonia kept talking with the moon. On winter nights, spring nights, summer nights. Until autumn came again. The ground was covered with leaves, we went back to school. Where is Antonia tonight? I can't hear her, somebody said. We can't hear her, we said. Antonia went to the moon, a little girl told us, I saw her going up. But then again, in the middle of the autumn, we started to hear Antonia. Is that Antonia? Yes, but it was another Antonia talking with the moon, baking bread, coming to town. The parish priest wanted to be sure and asked her, what do you do the two or three nights right before, during and after the full moon? I talk with my friend, the moon, Antonia answered. The parish priest wanted to add, go and remember... but he remembered he had already said that, so he only said, ha!

And Antonia kept talking with the moon. We kept having holidays. Winter kept coming, spring kept coming too, and also the summer. Until the autumn when we wouldn't hear Antonia at the beginning. Then again, there she is talking with the moon! we would say. And it was another Antonia. And even another Antonia the following autumn. And another the following autumn. And there will be another, because more Antonias are coming every year to my town, in the middle of the autumn, to talk with the moon.

Grandma

Grandma closed the door and came to sit at the table. I just got a letter. They will put me in jail if I don't start a war, she said to my father, mother, aunt, uncle, sister, two other aunts, three cousins and me. How do you know, grandma? I just know, and she repeated, I just got an official letter. Then do it! my father replied, ordering her. I do not know how to do it, she said, I have only learned how to stop wars.

(When I later asked her who had taught her, she smiled and said she had been self-taught.) My uncle, who used to say he knew a lot about everything, added that a war was good for the economy, because it gave people work, brought much-needed foreign investments, controlled the population and cleaned the environment of weeds and insects that spread diseases. My grandma stared at him for a moment and nobody else said a word that evening. We all knew she had been a problem for the government out there in the capital, because she had stopped every single war the generals had tried to start against big countries and small countries for big reasons and small reasons.

Next morning a big car stopped at my grandmother's home. The driver got out, wearing no medals. Then a man in uniform wearing two medals stepped out of the car followed by another uniformed man wearing five medals and finally somebody very important in uniform wearing twenty medals. This one went directly to grandma who was sweeping the sidewalk. I order you to start a war! he said without even a "good morning." She stopped sweeping for a moment and told him, I only know how to stop a war and I have already told you that. If you can stop a war, you should also know how to start one, he replied, his tone still imperative. She looked him in the eye, no sir, they are two different things: that's why the opposite happens to you: many times you have known how to start a war but have not known how to stop it. He got into his car and all the rest did too. Before leaving he shouted at grandma, if you don't do it, you will be arrested and put in jail!

Dios mío!!! We were all scared, and the neighbors who looked through their windows were too. Nobody had ever screamed at grandma, much less threatened her with arrest. Grandma in prison (what an injustice!): I could not stand the thought of it. My cousins couldn't either, my mother and Pedro the baker either, Matilde and don Pablo either. Grandma, the first teacher in the town, my first teacher. The woman who had brought the letters and numbers to the people. The woman who had brought the lights of education and twelve multiplied by nine is… (you guess). Grandma, the woman who had taken me to the Andes, the most magnificent mountains in the world (after lunch when others were taking a siesta); who had made me swim in the Atlantic, so deep and wide (at a time when I hadn't even dreamed of swimming); and who had told me the incredible story of a huge horse full of soldiers, which I could never understand because I only understood a soldier with many horses. Grandma, who knew how to stop wars, a knowledge she had used several times, considering the frequency of generals running the government. But she would not share this knowledge with anybody. Why should others have to carry the sorrow that I do, she used to say.

This time grandma had to do something: those generals in the capital could harm her family and the town. They had a lot of weapons and rumors were spreading that they were getting more from the north. Grandma did something: she put on her best dress (the one my mother had made for her), her new shoes (forever new because she never wore them), and asked my uncle to take her to the capital. She was going to talk to the twenty-medal general. What she told him was this: after thinking all day and night and at dawn too, a simple idea has come to me. Simple, very simple, my general. Just write a nasty letter to the president from the country you want to fight against, saying, "Oh, you incompetent president, I am better than you and have more weapons, too. If you don't believe me, let's try and you will see what I can do." While grandma talked, somebody without medals typed. The general listened and approved, listened and signed the letter. He signed the letter and sent ten soldiers with it to the post office, after telling them it was an official letter and had to be sent certified.

Grandma and my uncle returned home. Is there going to be another war? we eagerly asked. For an answer, grandma asked if the chickens had been fed and the vegetable garden had been watered. That evening we heard on the news that ten soldiers had deserted from the army. There were rumors they had taken with them an important military document. Apparently they had fled in a huge wooden horse somebody had built for the carnival parade. Worst of all, their whereabouts were unknown. Who knows, they must have already left the country, grandma commented turning the radio off. We had dinner and for dessert my uncle had bought alfajores in the capital. You can't imagine how good they were! Later when grandma was knitting, as she did every night before going to bed, I saw her smile and asked her, what is it? She looked at me and said with a wink, nowadays horses are built to stop wars before they begin rather than to win them.

Matilde

Matilde raised her head and looked at her rival. There she was, beautiful Dutch Eva, just come to my town. She had been brought all the way across the ocean in a ship especially commissioned for her. The queen, Matilde thought, had arrived in the capital's port and from there had come in a special train with guards, doctors, authorities and even a lawyer, to my town. Matilde, don't feel intimidated, the children said. We had been her supporters since the first time she competed four years ago at don Pablo's farm, because at that time the town didn't have the facilities to host such a competition. In the last few years, the town had prepared itself for such events and had gained national recognition when the president of the country declared it: "The capital of dairy products." The president himself was expected to attend this fierce competition between our Matilde and the Dutch Eva. All the town's authorities: the mayor (and his wife), the police chief (and his wife), the director of the post office (and his wife), the president of the Farmers' Association (and his wife) and the parish priest (and his assistant) were going to be part of the jury along with several foreigners and city people. We, the town's people, were too. Because during these events, the town was flooded with milk. Everyone was forced to drink it, taste it, look at it, and talk about it. And to make shakes, yogurt and cheese. It was the time when my mother, along with other mothers, would make flan six times a day for a week. It was the time that had inspired our mayor to declare flan the town's official dessert, now and forever.

Matilde and Eva were taken to the stable. Matilde walked, surrounded by children who cheered for her. Eva was taken in a special truck with her manager and her personal doctor checking her pulse and blood pressure and giving her small sips of mineral water brought in for her from Holland. Both were milked by the best farmers who ever lived in my town. The first verdict was that the foreigner's milk was superior. What a terrible shock for our Matilde, proud cow of our prairies! Don't feel intimidated, we told her again, what do these foreigners and city people know? Can they know more than our director of the post office, more than don Pablo, more than our mothers? No way! Matilde, born on a rainy day with Pepe's and María's help. Raised in the meadows where the horizon can never be reached. Fed with grasses from our fresh pastures, grasses tasty as the flan my mother made with her milk. Matilde, don't give up, you are our pride, you are our queen.

They were milked again. This time the verdict was that both were even in quality. But the next day was going to be the last trial. That night we couldn't sleep. We knew Eva, beautiful Dutch Eva, was being taken care of by a troop of professionals and was being given a reception by the president, traitor to our national cause. We, the children, met at the town plaza and organized a celebration for Matilde. We knocked at Juan the violinist's door, and at Paula's, the soprano who sang in the Sunday mass. We asked doña Rosa to give us some vegetables and Antonia to pray to the moon for justice. We took some stars to light our way and out we went to the stable. There Matilde was, resting and thinking. Cheer up sweet friend, here are some vegetables and songs and a poem Graciela wrote for you. We sat around her, singing and laughing. The night was as warm as Matilde's milk. That night of waiting... Until the next day arrived. It arrived when the roosters sang the morning song dedicated to Matilde. It arrived when the parish priest's assistant rang the bells and it was 7. You, who are sleeping! Get up, have some coffee with milk, take your banners and balloons and run to the stable! The jury was already trying Matilde's and Eva's milk. Even. Impossible! Try again. Even. Milk them again! They taste the same. One more time, please! It's the same... No, it's not the same!

Matilde's milk had gold nuggets in it. She was milked again while we jumped and laughed. Her milk had gold nuggets! It's beautiful! some people said. It will bring us a fortune! the president of the country exclaimed. And the jury proclaimed: best milk in the world: Matilde's.

That evening, there were fireworks and people danced. We made a crown of flowers for Matilde's head. Eva and her people left who knows when. Nobody saw them leaving. We were busy watching the mayor give Matilde the town's key. Matilde, born on a rainy day with Pepe's and María's help. Raised in the meadows where the horizon can never be reached. Fed with grasses from our fresh pastures, grasses tasty as the flan my mother made with her milk.

That year was actually Matilde's last competition. From then on she lived at don Pablo's farm, with the sun passing by, the nights passing by, the seasons passing by, and reading the classics.

Paula

On those dark nights when the stars seemed so tiny and far away, Paula, the soprano, sang. Paula, the soprano, sang and the stars came closer, looked bigger and illuminated the night like a hundred full moons. Some took advantage of this and went out searching for lost things. My aunt found one of her earrings under a tree. My father found two eggs that

Florencia, the youngest hen, had laid in the bushes instead of in the chicken coop. Tito found a plum fallen from the plum tree in the plaza. (Had it fallen in the morning? Had it fallen in the evening? He couldn't tell.) My brother found the smallest piece of time ever seen in my town on a branch of the eucalyptus tree across from señora Teresa's forbidden house. The parish priest found several sins hidden in his front yard: he felt ashamed, put them in his pockets and went inside the church.

Sometimes, Paula, the soprano, who also sang in the Sunday mass, would sing Schubert's Ave Maria and Mary (that is, Joseph's wife and Jesus' mother) would appear on top of the church tower smiling and blessing the town. People would look up, ooooohhhhh! they would exclaim, delighted. All the young brides-to-be would run home to put their wedding gowns on and go to the plaza across from the church to ask Mary for a special blessing to ensure they be solicitous wives. All the young men would also go and look up at Mary, since it was rumored she was the most beautiful woman on earth and in the whole universe. Lisa, Javier and I would go to the plaza too, and wave our hands to Mary, excited to finally meet her.

Until the parish priest ordered Paula to stop singing so Mary would stop blessing. According to the priest, Mary was doing something she was not supposed to do: only men were authorized to give blessings. (In his Sunday sermon, the parish priest repeated this fact to his flock, warning about creating more sins that would increase the already long list of existing ones.)

Paula, on those dark nights when the stars seemed so tiny and far away, sang. She sang and the stars came closer and my town seemed to be sheltered under the light of a hundred full moons. Sometimes, Paula would sing a lullaby and children would fall asleep immediately, even if they weren't in bed yet, even if they were sitting on the toilet, brushing their teeth or playing cards with their great-aunts. Some mothers then would ask her, sing again a lullaby tonight, Paula, and she would sing again a lullaby. Then, mothers and children, fathers and cousins, aunts and nieces would fall asleep, and the town would be one big silence, one big dream. Except, of course, for those searching for their misplaced thoughts and lost umbrellas.

Then one day, a day like any other in the town, Paula, who lived with her mother, announced she was going to stop singing at night because her mother was sick and even a lullaby woke her up. Her mother, who had taught Paula how to sing and had once won a singing competition in a nearby town, was in bed, with a temperature, having broth and mint tea. We are sorry for your mother, everyone said, may she get well soon. It has been so pleasant to have the stars near us, find our winter shoes, see Mary, find out where our cats hide at night and have our children sleeping well!

My aunt Angélica, who didn't sing in the Sunday mass, but sang whenever she was hanging clothes in her yard, told Paula, ask Mary, the wisest woman on earth, to bless your mother and the illness will go away. The parish priest warned them that Mary would need a special permit from him who would need a special permit from the bishop who would need a special permit from the pope. This process could take a long time and there was no certainty of getting the permit. Antonia, ah irreverent Antonia, who talked with the moon! encouraged Paula to bring some light from the moon to her mother instead. You must avoid all that bureaucracy, she said, come with me and get some light from my friend.

And Paula did so. The next day her mother stopped having a temperature. In the evening when Paula was singing a gratitude song to the moon, her mother got up, sat at the kitchen table and had soup and bread. The next day Paula's mother got up again, smiled and went out. We saw her watering her garden and walking to Pedro's bakery.

Paula then continued singing at night. On those dark nights when the stars seemed so tiny and far away, she sang. Paula sang and the stars came closer, looked bigger and illuminated the night like a hundred full moons. People continued searching for their lost things. My aunt Emilia, the clown, found her red nose under a cauliflower in my grandma's vegetable garden. Javier found his math homework he was sure he hadn't done, under a brick in the police station's front yard. The parish priest kept finding sins hidden in his front yard and spent a night writing a fierce anti-sin sermon to his flock. Esther was the luckiest of all. She found her memories: the memories she and her husband had managed to rescue when they fled from that far away land across the ocean. I found nothing relevant. I went every night to look for Florencia's eggs in the bush but she had laid them in the chicken coop.

Until one night, I found Mary sitting behind the bush and when I was just about to exclaim, Oh! she put her index finger to her lips and told me, sshhh! I am on my way to New Zealand but stopped here to rest. I am going to bless you all, but don't tell the priest. I think he doesn't understand what women can do.

I never learned how long Mary stayed in New Zealand, or the purpose of her trip, but our Paula continued singing at night. We continued finding a great variety of lost things. And with Paula and our findings, we felt blessed. On those dark nights when the stars seemed so tiny and far away, Paula, the soprano, sang. Paula sang and we felt blessed under the stars coming closer, looking bigger and illuminating the night like a hundred full moons.

Aurora

There was a man in our town who hated animals. All kinds of animals: small and big, long and short, green and red. Animals with wings to fly and animals without wings to fly. Animals with four legs and animals with three legs, if there were any. Animals who laughed all day long and animals who cried all night long. Animals who talked and animals who refused to talk. Frogs and kangaroos, llamas and lizards, whales and unicorns, octopi and roosters. He had tried to mobilize people for his organization: Citizens Against Animals. At first, he got some support from the town's religious authority, the parish priest, who was tired of seeing four dogs and the neighbors' hens attend mass on Sunday morning. The director of the post office had also considered joining: he didn't like the little pigs in his office who used to go from my uncle's backyard to the post office's backyard and from there into his building. But these potential supporters soon abandoned Citizens Against Animals when they realized the lack of popular support it would have in our town, since most inhabitants had from one to several animals, depending on whether she/he was a teacher, a baker, a farmer or something else.

When doña Rosa and Aurora came to live in our town and took the house next door to the one where the man full of hatred (as we had decided to call him) lived, they didn't suspect how much pain and sorrow they would have to endure. Doña Rosa used to work in the garden all morning and then go out to sell her vegetables. Aurora spent a lot of time perched on a bench on the sidewalk talking to people and singing, sometimes arias from famous operas, sometimes softer melodies. The man full of hatred left very early in the morning and came back when Aurora and doña Rosa were inside having dinner. He hadn't had the chance to meet them yet.

Until one day, he came home early. As he was opening the front door, he heard someone greeting him from the sidewalk. Hello, Aurora said, so polite and well-mannered she was. Hello, he answered. You came back early today, she added. He turned his head and was about to explain why he had come home early when he saw Aurora in person for the first time. A parrot! he exclaimed horrified, a disgusting, one-hundred-colored parrot perched on a bench on the sidewalk! And I greeted it! He rushed inside and double locked his door. He waited until dark to go out. Then to the police he went. There is a parrot next to my house, he stated with indignation. The policeman already knew about his hatred so he looked at him and said, do you want to place any charges against her? I want it arrested and put in jail, the man answered, more indignant than ever. We can't do that, unless she has done something terrible to you. It insulted me… and threatened me!

Doña Rosa was washing dishes after dinner when the police came and said that Aurora had to be taken to jail. Aurora couldn't believe her neighbor would place charges against her. She asked what the charges were. Insults and threats, the policeman answered, and even though the law says you can call a lawyer, we don't follow the law that strictly. Aurora was trying to comprehend the situation. There is no parrot in the whole world who has ever threatened any living creature, she firmly stated. Doña Rosa, still shocked by such an unexpected happening, told Aurora better not to resist the police. You should go with him, she said, it undoubtedly is a mistake, we are peaceful inhabitants, tomorrow everything will be cleared up and you will be back home.

As it turned out, Aurora didn't have a bad time at the police station. They soon realized they couldn't keep her behind bars, so she spent the night perched on a chair talking with the two policemen on guard and continued talking with the only prisoner who was behind bars, after the policemen fell asleep. It was through this man that she learned about her neighbor. He is a strange man, he told her, I heard he was stung by a wasp when he was thirteen and ever since then he has hated animals. This is very serious, Aurora thought. She had never confronted hatred before.

Aurora was released without bail in the evening of the following day because her behavior had been exemplary. Perched on a chair, she had sung the prisoner's favorite songs, given good advice to drunk men arrested in the street, taught a policeman how to make thin crust pizza and answered the phone when the police chief and the officers were taking their afternoon nap. She also offered to read the paper aloud, but nobody was interested in knowing what was going on beyond the town. When she came back home, doña Rosa was already organizing the neighbors to defend Aurora against the man full of hatred. He, on the other hand, was unsuccessfully trying to organize neighbors against Aurora and doña Rosa.

She is the only one who talks to me when I am cleaning the streets, the man who cleaned the streets said. She insults people, the man full of hatred replied. I hear her singing when I am hanging washed clothes in my yard and her melodies make my good memories come and dance around me, said a woman who lived across the street from Aurora. She disturbs the neighborhood with her squawking, the man full of hatred replied. She tells us jokes when we pass by, several children testified: we go and tell them to the teachers and the school fills with laughter. She scares people with her malicious stories, the man full of hatred replied. I have stopped getting drunk thanks to her advice, said a man who Aurora met at the police station. She shits on the sidewalk, the man full of hatred replied. The judge had a rather easy time with Aurora's case: all the things said in her favor could be proven, all the charges placed against her could not... except that last one.

Aurora, the one-hundred-colored parrot, was allowed to return to her normal life once doña Rosa put some sort of bedpan under the bench where she perched every day. It also was the end for the man full of hatred. That is, the end of his life in our town. He left early one morning and never returned. We heard rumors that he had moved to Antarctica because he thought (erroneously, of course) that there were fewer animals there, and absolutely no parrots and no wasps.

Emilia

Emilia was a clown. A clown with painted face, red nose (which she had lost, and then found in my grandma's vegetable garden thanks to Paula's singing), big smile and enormous shoes. A little bit like other clowns I had seen in magazines and once in a circus that came to the town, stayed for a week and left. My great-aunt Emilia was the town's official clown. She delivered speeches, jumped rope, walked on a string

from roof to roof (we were breathless), climbed the church tower and on top stood on one foot, ate watermelon and smoked a pipe (we were breathless). She flew on a bicycle with wings landing on the river where the ducks swam away complaining quack-quack-quack. My great-aunt Emilia rode a big wooden horse to the plaza and there stood up on top and played the saxophone (we and the wooden horse were breathless). A clown is a clown, a clown is not supposed to do all those things you do, her sister, my grandma, told her one day. But I do all those things, Emilia answered, because not only do I want people to laugh but also to be astonished and say
"oooooooooooooooooh." We all certainly said
"ooooooooooooooooooooooooooooooooh"
for so long that sometimes she had already finished her performance and we remained saying
"ooooooooooooooooh."

One day, Antonia came and told Emilia, there is a girl who lives with her mother in a hut just outside the town, near my hut. She is very sad and her mother doesn't know what to do. I am praying to the moon for her, but would you come and help her and make her laugh? Emilia put on her costume, her enormous shoes, her big smile, her red nose, painted her face and walked to the girl's hut. She saw the girl outside, silent and sad. I am very sad, she told Emilia, I would like to eat something, sleep at night and go to see you in the town plaza, but I don't feel like moving and I can hardly talk. I cannot even remember why I am so sad. My great-aunt Emilia, the town's official clown, told the girl to wait a moment, she was going to go and get her bicycle with wings and they were going for a ride. The girl smiled. She forgot she had been sad and started to jump up and down saying, I will fly, I will fly. Our clown Emilia came back riding her bike. She then unfolded its wings, mounted the girl on the bike's handlebars and up they went. The girl saw the town (we saw them and were breathless), the fields with the corn ready to harvest, the cows having lunch and Matilde teaching don Pablo how to improve the milking system. She saw Paula, the soprano who sang in the Sunday mass, sitting in her backyard making copies by hand of a new song for the birds. She saw grandma, who refused to be breathless, working in her vegetable garden. She saw Carolina planting trees and Antonia selling her bread. You see, Emilia told her, there is a lot to enjoy. Forget your sadness, she continued, as you have forgotten it now, and you will see Antonia talking with the moon, the stars coming closer when Paula sings at night, the birds taking their places on the trees for their morning song and you will see me, walking on a string from roof to roof and eating watermelon on top of the church tower. They flew for hours (we got used to seeing them above us all afternoon and started to breathe again). When they finally landed, near the hut, the girl said, I remember now why I have been sad. And then she asked Emilia, can you answer this question: why do my mother and I live in this hut we are afraid the wind will blow it down, and you and other people live in the town, in houses with vegetable gardens, in houses with electricity, in houses made of bricks? Emilia was silent. For the first time in her career as a clown, Emilia could not answer. She told the girl she would come back and give her another ride. She pondered and pondered over the question, until one day she began to paint her face with tears falling down from her eyes. The tears slowly erased her big smile and Emilia became a sad-faced clown. Very much like other clowns I had seen in magazines and in a circus that came once to the town, stayed for a week and left.

The Two Antonias

One autumn, we had two Antonias at the same time. That was the autumn of abundance. Fresh bread twice a day. I bought bread from Antonia this morning, said the woman who delivered the paper in the afternoon which was when the paper arrived in town. My aunt Angélica, who was picking up the clothes she had hung in the morning, replied, come and try this bread. I've just bought it from Antonia, or from another Antonia I am not sure, and it tastes different from this morning's bread, even the shape is different.

That was the autumn when neighboring towns also declared holidays during the full moon: so loud were our two Antonias' simultaneous conversations. People from those towns enjoyed the talk, that is, the sound of the talk. They also enjoyed having extra holidays. And they wanted to try the two Antonias' breads: come here Antonias, come here to sell your bread! they called over the green pastures. But the mayors of our neighboring towns started to worry about this situation that they considered to be unusual, and came to our mayor to ask how it could happen.

What? our mayor asked, half-asleep, because he had been awakened at eleven in the morning on a holiday. How could this happen? they repeated, to have two Antonias, two Antonias talking with the moon! Our mayor didn't have the answer. This type of situation is not under my jurisdiction, he told them, but then he remembered he had heard the woman who swept the autumn leaves in the plaza say it had to do with the seasons. Sometimes you have two seasons at the same time, she said and the mayor said to the mayors. Two seasons at the same time! they all exclaimed, we are clearly having autumn now! How can I know? our mayor complained, irritated, how can I know? he repeated, maybe we are having two autumns! One autumn brings Antonia, two autumns should bring two Antonias, they all said in unison. They finally understood, and felt relieved. That explanation seems correct to me, but there must be something else, the most skeptical of the mayors said, and he asked, who, did you say, was that person who knows about the seasons? The woman who sweeps the plaza, our mayor answered, but Carolina knows too, and so do doña Rosa and Aurora, well, I am not sure about Aurora, but Eva and Paula and Emilia and… That's enough! they stopped him. It seems a lot of people know things you don't know, a particularly envious and malicious mayor told ours (because after all, to have two autumns and two Antonias was a reason for pride… and envy!).

They decided to ask Carolina. She wasn't at home. She is planting trees on the outskirts of town, her son Javier said when he opened the door. They went to doña Rosa. She was working in her garden. It's simple, she said, sometimes there is an overlapping of seasons or one season forgets it has already arrived in this part of the world and it comes again. Then, we get the same season double at the same time. This is what is going on right now with the two autumns. But, this doesn't happen often, so there won't be two Antonias for too long. By the end of these autumns, one of the Antonias will go away, she concluded and added, you will miss hearing her sound and having her bread, won't you? because one Antonia can't be as loud as two and she will bake bread only for our town. The mayors left. They were confused. I've always said that it is hard to govern a town, one of them sighed. What seems to be clear is that there will be only one Antonia soon, another commented and realized, no more extra holidays!

And so it happened: one night we heard one Antonia talking with the moon. The next day, nobody made any comments when she came in the afternoon to sell her bread. Some people from neighboring towns complained: no more Antonias!, no more bread!, no more holidays! We told them, wait until next year, it might happen again. But, as far as I can recall, it never happened again. The cycle of seasons kept coming just one after the other with one season each time. The cycle of Antonias kept coming just one after the other. A new Antonia in the new autumn and we would start all over again. There she is! There she is! There she is! We would start all over again.

Carolina

Let the leaves be on the trees! Javier's mother told him. He used to pull the leaves off the trees and never put them back. Javier's mother was Carolina, the woman who planted trees. Trees were pleased to be planted. Birds were pleased that trees were planted. The mayor's wife was pleased that birds were pleased that trees were planted. But the mayor was not pleased. Too many trees, I am the mayor of a forest, not a town! he complained. We need trees for the birds, we need birds for the music, Carolina said. His answer would be that we had enough music with Paula. Carolina would remind him that Paula only sang at night and in the Sunday mass. We need music during the day, she would add, so children can walk to school happily… I can't write my memos with all that music! – older people will enjoy working in their gardens – I can't dictate my letters! – the bread will be tastier because don Pedro the baker and Antonia, who also makes bread, will be delighted with the birds' melodies – I can't read the paper! – our milk will continue being the best in the world because birds will entertain the cows while they are being milked – I can't, I can't, I can't, he would reply, reply, reply.

But one day somebody important was coming to town. I don't remember who he was but I know he was somebody important because the mayor needed a band to play the national anthem. Carolina, could you plant more trees in the plaza so birds will come and sing? he asked. You have been complaining about the music and now…, she tried to say. The town doesn't have a band, he interrupted her, and I need somebody to play or sing the national anthem! Birds won't do that! Carolina assured him. Why not? – because they don't like any expression of nationalism – it will be an order! – they don't have citizenship - they could be arrested! – or ID or birth certificate or passport from any country - they could be put in jail! – nor do they consider themselves legal or illegal residents - they are in my territory and I can expel them all! Carolina, a witty woman, calmed him down. My dear mayor, she started, let the birds sing something else, it will be different and, I don't want to sound disrespectful, but our visitor might be tired of hearing the national anthem everywhere he goes. And so, Carolina went and planted more and more trees in the plaza where the reception was going to take place. Between you and me, I thought the plaza looked like a forest. My cousins Marta and Rodolfo thought so too and my friend Javier, Carolina's son, thought so too.

But trees were planted and the day of the reception arrived with five thousand birds perched on their branches, small and big, that is, small branches and big branches, small birds and big birds. What a commotion when, at Carolina's signal, they started to sing, "Miren cómo nos hablan de libertad/ cuando de ella nos privan en realidad," a Violeta Parra song, sung in Spanish, "Miren cómo pregonan tranquilidad/ cuando nos atormenta la autoridad/ ¿Qué dirá el santo Padre que vive en Roma,/ que le están degollando a sus palomas?"* The parish priest was furious, Carolina shook her arms to stop them, the mayor talked to the visitor, apologetic, and we laughed and laughed until the birds stopped. At Carolina's second signal, they started again, but this time with "The hills are alive/ with the sound of music," sung in English, because, besides singing in their own languages, they sang in many different human languages, except Danish, which seemed to be too difficult for them.

The visitor was delighted, particularly because the song was sung in English, even though he couldn't understand a word. But after he left, the mayor went to Carolina and asked to uproot all the trees in the plaza, all the trees in the town, and all the trees on the outskirts. Birds have become subversives, he said, what was all that singing about authority and freedom? They don't know what a headache it is to run this town! I think they were addressing the song to our visitor, Carolina explained, and I want to clarify that I did not know what songs they were planning to sing: I had given them complete freedom to choose from their repertoire. But in any case, my dear mayor, trees are not only for birds. They give us shade on those hot summer days, she continued, they give us the smell that announces spring, they give us the wind that takes dust and bad thoughts away, they give us rain for the river and the wells, they give us the calm of their green and the joy of their buds. I have to admit, admitted the mayor, that I need them for those hot summer days when I like to sit under their shade, and in winter, to use their dried branches for firewood... but what about the birds, Carolina? They must not sing protest songs. Perhaps Paula could teach them Schubert's Ave Maria.

But my friend Javier's mother was witty. My dear mayor, she said, as you well know, birds are birds, they don't have the laws and fears we do because their society or organization is not as developed as ours, that is, it is more primitive than ours. That's why we can't impose on them our rules, ideas, even habits. Ha! said the mayor, I hadn't thought about that, they are truly inferior to us, we, mankind, are the most advanced stage in evolution! Right, Carolina asserted, you, mankind, are the most advanced stage in evolution. And she continued planting trees. For whoever needed them. Wherever they were needed. Carolina, could you come and plant two elms in my yard? Carolina, could you plant a maple next to my sidewalk?

The birds eventually formed a chorus that became the town's official chorus, conducted by Paula who prepared a wide repertoire which included "The Man I Love" and one of Bach's Masses (the easiest one). Birds continued singing songs by Violeta Parra, but they agreed not to do it on the occasion of official receptions. Paula convinced them to learn the national anthem, because she thought that after all, they might need to sing it on one of the country's holidays, and she spent a lot of time trying to teach it to them. Birds are used to traveling around the globe, north and south, east and west, so these ones had heard a great variety of national anthems, and they had picked up words and tunes from here and there, from this one and that one. When Paula was teaching them ours, they would start with New Guinea's anthem, continued with Tunisia's, switched to Portugal's, switched again to Belgium's and finish with Cuba's, all sung in their original languages. And what was remarkable is that they seemed to have fun mixing national anthems. Paula finally gave up, talked to the mayor and told him that it was impossible for the birds to learn to sing only our national anthem. They had learned ours but kept mixing it with several others (she didn't tell him that the birds seemed to enjoy mixing the anthems). The mayor understood that it wasn't appropriate to have the birds sing a potpourri of national anthems at official ceremonies or the country's holidays and accepted Paula's suggestion that they should sing one of the melodies they had learned instead.

Carolina administered the chorus. She had a special relation with the birds and they liked her very much. But she couldn't attend any of their rehearsals: she was usually busy planting trees here and there and sometimes she even went to other towns that needed trees and had requested her services. There were not many people who planted trees in those days. Carolina's fame as the woman who planted trees reached beyond the horizon. And the horizon was a long distance from my town!

* "Look how they talk about freedom/ when they are actually depriving us of it. Look how they talk about calm/ when the authority is tormenting us. What will the holy Father say/ he who lives in Rome/ that they are slashing the throats of his doves?"

Violeta Parra: ¿Qué dirá el santo Padre? (What Will The Holy Father Say?)

Eva

Eva did not speak with the moon. Eva did not sing beautiful songs. Eva never brought the stars closer and made the night brighter. Eva did not plant trees or fly on a bike or eat watermelon on the church's tower. Eva did not do any of these things. Eva, however, did something, otherwise I wouldn't talk about her. Eva told stories. She was the town storyteller. At sunset we used to sit in the plaza, making a circle around her. Eva, tell us the story of the woman with eleven eyes, somebody would ask. I've already told you that story eleven times! she would reply. Children especially liked to hear the same story over and over again and she liked to repeat it — changing settings, characters and, sometimes, the ending. Eva, you told us the girl flew on a horse and now you are saying she flew on an eagle! Javier or somebody else would say. I could have never said the girl flew on a horse because horses don't have wings, Eva would reply.

A long time ago and far away a man swallowed a whale and got indigestion, Eva started. He had thought it was a big trout, but no, it was a whale, a whale who became upset because she didn't want to be swallowed. We have never seen a whale, we all said. Let's go to the river, Eva replied. I saw one there this morning. Wait a minute, I said, you mean in the river made by the woman who made a river? We don't have any other river around here, Eva looked at me and gave me a wink. Why did she give me a wink? (I guess I learned why much later.)

Some men sitting on a bench in the plaza looked at us walking to the river and commented, Eva is taking the children for a walk to the river. She invents all these stories and has told them there is a whale in the river. They all laughed. A whale in a river! Impossible! Besides that river doesn't even have a single trout! But when we arrived, we saw the shiny black back of a huge, long animal. The river was starting to flood… We got scared. We got scared that the river started to flood. Eva calmed us down. She said that there wouldn't be a flood because the whale was leaving soon because the ducks were quacking at her and anyway she preferred the depth and vastness of the sea. I have never seen an animal so big! I said. Could we ride her for a while? Marta asked. Only for a while because she has to leave, Eva answered and called to the whale, come closer, we would like to get on your back! The whale came closer and we got on her back. Eva, tell us another story! somebody said when we were all on board.

There was once a whale, she started, a whale in a river, can you believe it?! The ducks were angry because they said she had taken their territory, and they couldn't swim, quack, quack, quack. But the children of a nearby town enjoyed riding the whale and listening to a crazy old woman telling the story of a whale that took the children for a ride and disturbed the ducks, because they wanted the river for themselves, naturally, they had been there first. What about the man who swallowed the whale? Lisa asked. Well, Eva continued, he swallowed the whale, the children, and the crazy woman telling the story of a whale that almost flooded the river. That's scary! we said. Yes, it was, Eva replied, but only for a while because the whale was going to leave, leave for the deep and vast sea and the sea was waiting for her. What about the man who swallowed the whale, the children and the woman? Lisa insisted. What do you think? Eva asked. He got indigestion, we all said. Right, she agreed, he got indigestion and had to go to the doctor. Doctor and patient got really upset at the crazy woman who could be heard from the patient's belly telling stories to the children, Eva added.

Until the whale said, this has been a long ride! Eva, you and the children need to go home now. We all walked home because it was dark and night had fallen. The doctor told the man with indigestion to go home, Eva said, because it was dark and night had fallen. And she concluded, everyone went home, except for the whale. The whale went to the sea. The sea was happy to have the whale back. I have been waiting for you the whole story long! the sea said and gave her a big hug.

Eva, who did not speak with the moon, bring the stars closer or fly on a bike, told stories. On at least one occasion she took us for a ride on a whale. But never on a horse with wings, because, of course, horses don't have wings.

Lisa

Suddenly we saw an elephant in the plaza. People gathered around and observed her with astonished eyes. It was unusual. It was strange. She was a real one: big ears, four legs, a huge trunk... Who brought it here? somebody asked. Lisa stepped forward and said, I did not bring her here, I made her appear... Look, with this handkerchief I can make her disappear. And the elephant was gone. We had no words to express our surprise. You are a magician! we all exclaimed. Aren't you the daughter of Enrique and Josefa, don Pedro's neighbor…? And a friend of Eva, the storyteller, Lisa added.

Lisa was only nine years old and she was already a magician. You didn't tell us anything about it! the children complained. I didn't know it myself, she replied, I found out two weeks ago when my mother put a bowl of vegetable soup in front of me for lunch, as she usually does. You know how much I dislike vegetable soup, so just for fun I took a handkerchief, covered the bowl with it and said, "I want this awful soup to be turned into a mountain of French fries," and you know what? It did! it turned into a mountain of French fries! Since then I have been having a lot of French fries, some cheese, and chocolate cake for lunch, and my mom doesn't know anything about it.

Lisa should have never revealed her lunches, because every single child who heard the story went to her/his mom and asked her, could we invite Lisa over for lunch? I did it, too. After all, I was a good friend of hers, and the mashed potatoes my mom had made were turned into a mountain of French fries when Lisa came over for lunch. French fries? my brother asked when he came into the kitchen. I saw Lisa pulling out her handkerchief and saying, "no, mashed potatoes!" We didn't touch the mashed potatoes until he left, then we continued having French fries. It was during lunch that I suggested Lisa do magic shows in the plaza. She agreed and added, we should charge and use the money to buy the textbooks for the children at school who can't afford them.

Lisa started to give one or two shows a week. Children had a lot of fun and adults did, too. Until she got in trouble with the police. One afternoon two policemen were enjoying the show, when Lisa came down from the stage and walked among the audience, as she did in every show. Sirs, I am going to do some magic on you, she told the policemen, and covered them with her handkerchief. When she uncovered them, they looked the same, except their guns were missing. Lisa couldn't bring their guns back. The two policemen were very upset and cancelled all her shows. You cannot make fun of the authorities, the parish priest told Lisa. On a Sunday morning, during mass, she had turned a statue of saint Paul into a young woman with a long dress carrying an umbrella. The priest had been very embarrassed until Lisa's mother ordered her to bring back saint Paul and she did so. Now, her shows were cancelled.

What can we do? a child asked. Let's have shows in my home basement, Javier said. Carolina, his mother, was busy planting trees here and there and we assigned Octavio, his dog, to keep guard upstairs and bark when somebody was approaching. But we couldn't buy more textbooks because no adults came to our shows in the basement and the children didn't have money. Lisa then decided to go to the plaza by herself and bring back the elephant, the huge elephant who started to step on the bushes and eat the flowers. You have to make this elephant disappear, the mayor and the police told her. Only if you let me have my shows here again, she replied. This is such a spoiled child, the mayor commented, while the elephant scooped up his hat with her trunk and threw it on top of the flag pole. Lisa went on, I need to continue my shows and earn money to buy the textbooks for the children at school who cannot afford them. On top of that, she is a communist! one of the policemen exclaimed. The mayor and his wife decided to talk with Lisa's parents. But Lisa's parents felt they couldn't do much. She very much wants to help some children at school, her mother said. The mayor threatened them, you have to pay a fine! And they had to. The next day there were two elephants in the plaza. If you make my parents pay more fines, you will see more elephants in the plaza, Lisa said. There were no bushes and flowers left, so the second elephant, smaller than the first one, crossed the street and went into the church, which always keeps its doors open for the parishioners. She went to church and ate the chrysanthemums for saint Peter, the carnations for saint Francis, the daisies for baby Jesus and the roses for Mary. She drank the water from the baptismal font and returned to the plaza taking on her trunk the big candle holder the priest had left at the door. The priest thought of the man who hated animals: gone, in Antarctica perhaps, without elephants and spoiled children… If only he could be here! he sighed. But he wasn't there and the battle was lost. Let the child have her shows at the plaza! he begged the

53

mayor and the police. The best thing to do is to have a vote, a popular vote, somebody suggested, do people want the shows or not? There were only seven votes against the shows at the plaza: the mayor and his wife, the police chief, the two policemen still furious and the two elephants who didn't want to disappear.

The next day Lisa started her shows again. Her first trick was to make one elephant disappear. In her second trick, the second elephant was gone, taking with her the big candle holder from the church. For her third trick, she asked the audience for a hat. I need a nice, expensive hat, she said, it has to be very expensive. The mayor's wife, who was attending the show in order to improve relations with the children, offered hers pointing out that it had been designed by a famous hat designer who lived in Paris. Lisa took the hat, put it on the table, covered it with her handkerchief and pronounced some magic words. When she pulled off her handkerchief, six books appeared on the table and the hat was gone. What books are those? we asked, knowing the answer. These are the textbooks for Clara and Estela, Julio and Carola, Beto and Raúl, she answered, and they could only come from a very expensive hat. Thank you, mayor's wife! all the children exclaimed. You're welcome, she said and left in a hurry.

Lisa continued offering shows long after everyone had her/his textbook. Once a circus came to town and stayed for a week. When it was leaving, the manager asked Lisa to come with them. She said no, I just do this for fun, I do not want to become a circus star. When I am older, I want to study other cultures, go to China, play the violin and be a chef. But that will be later. Now I am fine being who I am.

The Time
The Town Went Dark

This was the time when we thought the moon had disappeared. For two consecutive months: no moon. Small or big. Waxing or new. Full or waning. Nothing. Just a hole in the sky. What have you done to the moon? we asked Antonia, who, as you already know from two previous stories, used to talk with the moon. Have you said something that upset her? Go and ask the parish priest, Antonia replied. He sent the moon a letter requesting that she never show up again. He said our nighttime conversations were disturbing the town. This was the type of thing we, humans and animals, didn't like: the parish priest getting involved in issues not directly related to his church. It's true that there was a bit of a public disturbance every full moon: Antonia and the moon would talk very loudly, and would keep talking for hours at a time when people were usually sleeping. Or so we should have been, but we couldn't sleep, and the next day we the children fell asleep on our desks at school, and people fell asleep at work, in the street, in a park, in the church. But we didn't mind these disturbances: there was something marvelous about the conversations, and the light and beauty of the night.

A neighborhood committee was formed, and went to talk with the priest. God asked me to do that, was the priest's answer. Could you please tell God to change his mind? the committee demanded, we can't live without the moon, no people on earth can live without her! The priest was adamant: No! he said. In all fairness, we never believed God had asked the priest to do such an ungodly thing, but considering the committee's failure, we children decided to organize the resistance. The moon had to come back. The moon had to talk with Antonia, yes, but also to be with us. The whole town was starting to wither without her light and beauty. Animals couldn't move without her company.

Thanks to Antonia, a group of us went to the fields to have a secret meeting with the moon. Matilde, Aurora and Octavio also attended. The parish priest wrote to me and told me he was representing the people's will, the moon said to the group. (This was the type of thing we didn't like, the parish priest saying he represented the people's will.) We all asked her to come back for the humans' and animals' sake. What if he calls the armed forces to shoot me? the moon said, concerned. The armed forces wouldn't do that because they know that the international outcry would be overwhelming, we reassured her.

After days of thinking and uncertainty, one night Antonia heard the moon calling her. Tell the town I'll come back for everyone but the parish priest, he won't be able to see me or hear my voice, the moon told her. And that was what happened. The moon started to come again to our town. First, new. Then, waxing. Then, full. And finally, waning. That is, in the same way and order she had always been coming to the town, and to many other towns in the world, I suppose. Antonia kept talking loudly with her when the moon was full, and we kept sleeping in on those mornings when the night before had been so bright and full of sounds we couldn't and didn't want to sleep. The parish priest thought our sleeping patterns had hopelessly gone wrong. For a moment, he thought of enacting a decree that would name it a sin to sleep in the morning, but he was afraid of losing parishioners (he had already lost many).

Things remained like that until the parish priest realized he couldn't survive without the moon, and lifted the ban. He sent another letter to the moon saying God was willing to let her come back to the town, could you please come back? The moon had so much fun with that letter that although she was waning, she exploded in laughter and became full again. She told Antonia about the letter, Antonia told us, and the town and the moon were one big fit of laughter. The parish priest heard us laughing, so he also laughed, but he didn't know why he was laughing.

On that night, when the breeze was cool and we all knew autumn was returning.

Just A Little Scare (Aurora, again)

On Wednesday at 9pm, somebody knocked at the door. Doña Rosa stopped washing the dishes, dried her hands on her apron and went to open it. It had been a short time since the events with the man full of hatred had taken place. A short time. Now somebody knocked at the door at 9pm. Doña Rosa went cautiously to open it. Aurora remained cautiously perched on a chair.

We are a photographer and a reporter from *El Tiempo*, two men standing at the door said. What do you want? doña Rosa asked, not very politely and without letting them in. Ask them to show you their credentials, Aurora advised from the back. The two started again, we are a photographer and a reporter from *El Tiempo*, the largest paper in the capital city. Somebody stopped by our office a short time ago and told us he had had to leave his home and his town because the devil, disguised as a parrot, had come to live next door. It took us a long time to find your town, it's not located on any map, and when we finally found it, we didn't know how to find your house because the man who came to our office didn't give us an address. We walked around the plaza, and everyone we asked, answered, "There is more than one parrot in the town, what do you mean by 'the one who speaks'? All of them talk!" Finally, we stopped at the police station and they said, "Ah, you mean Aurora!" they all laughed and told us to come here.

Doña Rosa laughed too, but Aurora didn't. She flew onto doña Rosa's shoulder and with great dignity told the men, I am not the devil. I am an ordinary, working class, rural, good-hearted parrot. I don't hurt anybody. I don't hate anybody. Prodigious! one of them exclaimed, you see how articulate this parrot is! The other asked, can we come in, do an interview and take some photos?

No interviews, no photos, nothing! Aurora exclaimed, rightly impatient, I am not the devil! Nor am I the holy spirit! I am a parrot! Doña Rosa tried to calm Aurora down. Then she told the men, you seem to come from a city where there are no parrots. Have you never heard a parrot talking? No? My dear reporter and my dear photographer, go back to where you came from. There is no news here. No news here! Aurora repeated. No news here, they repeated, and looked at each other. What is news for some people might not be news for others, they wisely decided, there seems to be nothing unusual here, this woman and her parrot, that's all, what a waste of time! And they left.

Doña Rosa closed the door and Aurora flew to the corner of the big old table where the big old radio was. She turned the radio on. It was getting late for the opera program on the classical station. There she had learned most of her arias. But when she heard, "tonight we are listening to *Tosca*," she was disappointed. Again! I already know *Tosca* by heart! she exclaimed. Doña Rosa smiled: the truth was that *Tosca* always moved Aurora to tears.

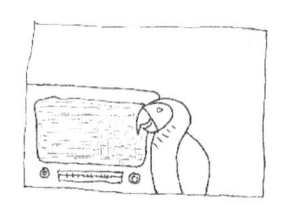

Victoria

There was alarm in the town when Victoria, the woman with a bow and an arrow, arrived. Both people and animals were alarmed. Rumors spread that she was a hunter. The man full of hatred would have been happy, somebody commented. But he was already gone. To the big city and then Antarctica, some said; nobody knows for sure, others said. Victoria, the woman with a bow and an arrow, had come to live in our town. I don't want to end up in a cage, Aurora thought, or cooked in a stew with potatoes and carrots! Matilde was also alarmed. She put her book aside and went to don Pablo, the farmer. I am not supposed to die a violent death, she told him. Don Pablo was also alarmed, but he smiled and patted her saying, don't worry. Relieved, she went back to reading Ovid's fables.

Somebody, though, thought he could make a deal with Victoria. The parish priest called her to his office and asked, Victoria, I've heard you are a hunter, could you hunt the hens and dogs that come into the church on Sunday morning when I am saying mass? I don't hunt hens and dogs, she replied. Oh! he exclaimed, surprised. Then, could you perhaps hunt the elephants if Lisa brings them again in the plaza? I don't hunt elephants, either, she said. In fact, I don't hunt any animal at all, she clarified, I catch the people who harm them. The parish priest stepped back. I am new to this town and many of you think I am a hunter, she added, but you have the wrong idea about me, you will see, you will see.

In the following weeks and months, Victoria caught two brothers who had been badly beating their horses. She caught a man from a neighboring town who was shooting down ducks in the river. She caught somebody throwing garbage into the river, polluting its water and killing its fish. She caught a policeman using pigeons for target practice outside the town. She rescued Toby, my grandma's cat, who had fallen into a well... You might ask, what did she do with the people she caught? Well, don't expect me to say that she killed them. But she took and destroyed their weapons. She also reprimanded the perpetrators and made them swear they would not mistreat animals again. The policeman complained, you took my gun but I am part of the authority. You don't have any authority to kill pigeons, she replied and walked away.

Victoria was a courageous woman, sweet, and gentle, too. She knew a lot about animals! Big and small. Green and red. Winged and not winged. Polite and impolite. Fierce and cowardly. She once came to our school and told us everything about them. I like elephants, Lisa said when Victoria finished her talk, but I can only make them appear on the outskirts of the town. Lisa had signed a peace treaty with the mayor, which stated, among other things, that she would not bring big animals to the plaza, except for special events. It was the mayor and his wife who suggested to Victoria to found an organization for the protection of animals and charge the town's people a special tax to fund it. The mayor's wife could be its president. Victoria strongly objected to creating a special tax. You should provide the funds, she told the mayor. The mayor said his office didn't have the money, and it was impossible to establish an organization without money. So, we didn't have an organization for the protection of animals.

After all, we had Victoria. She dedicated herself to watching over the members of all species other than humans. This activity kept her busy because, let's face it, there were abuses and incidents. Like when she had to intervene at a wedding in order to stop the bridegroom's aggression toward the bird chorus. The chorus had been singing at the outdoor summer wedding party, and the groom and his brother started to throw stones at them and at Paula who was, of course, conducting. Somebody called Victoria and she came immediately. The brothers had gotten upset because the chorus had been singing "Franqueza," a bolero in which a man tells a woman that he wants to be frank with her and break up because he doesn't love her anymore. The song couldn't have been more inappropriate for the occasion, but the birds and Paula didn't deserve to be stoned. According to witnesses, they were singing beautifully.

I remembered the day when Victoria met Aurora. It was a spring afternoon when I was coming back from school. I heard Aurora singing "O Sole Mio" and saw Victoria crossing the street to greet her. Aurora stopped singing. Nice to meet you, she said. Well, we have finally met, Victoria said, I heard a lot about you. I heard a lot about you, Aurora said back. Go on singing, Victoria asked her, go on, I like the song you were singing. Aurora went on, but she switched to an aria from Mme. Butterfly because she couldn't remember all the words from O Sole Mio. Victoria listened to her and I did too. We looked at each other and she told me, what a sweet parrot Aurora is! After I left, Victoria stayed a long time listening to Aurora singing. I heard that she sang as well as ever because, let's face it, Aurora loved to be a prima donna.

Perhaps Victoria's most remarkable action was to help a whale from one of Eva's stories leave our river and go back to the sea. That was in early March, I remember. We watched from the shore, said goodbye to the whale, and gave Victoria a standing ovation.

Victoria never left town, as far as I know. As many other women, except, as you well know, the woman who made a river, Victoria never left town. She never moved to the city or to another town. Like my grandma, and Antonia and Carolina, she came here and here she stayed, contributing to the well-being of everyone. Everyone who breathed, everyone who talked, everyone who sang, walked or ran, everyone who swam and everyone who flew. That's why she also contributed to the well-being of my aunt Emilia, the only woman in the town who flew.

As for her bow and arrow: after her arrival at our town, she never carried them again. She never used them either. I never asked her why she had them. But I didn't care, that's how it was and period.

The Moonlight Orange Tree

One afternoon, at the beginning of winter, Javier, his dog Octavio and I were looking at the orange tree in the church's front yard. It was so full of oranges that the whole tree looked rather orange in color with a few green spots. My mom planted it, Javier informed me. I wasn't surprised. Most of the trees in the town had been planted by her. These are the most beautiful oranges in town, Antonia commented. She was passing by with her basket full of fresh bread and stopped to talk with us. Carolina planted this orange tree one night, she said. I remember that night, under the full moon, a clear and joyful night. Carolina and I knew then that this tree was going to give the sweetest, juiciest and brightest oranges in town. And not only that, she added after a pause, it would also be the most abundant orange tree, providing oranges for the entire town… a very special tree.

Antonia, do you think we could try one? I asked her. I don't see why not, she answered. The parish priest came out from the church just when Javier and I were about to pick one orange each. What are you doing?! he shouted at us, don't you know you are not supposed to touch those oranges?! We thought we could, Javier and I said. Why can't they? Antonia asked. These oranges belong to the church, he answered her. I see, she said, so if they want to eat some, they need to ask you for a permit and you need to ask the bishop for a permit and he needs to ask the pope for a permit: all that can take a long time and there is no certainty of getting it. He didn't say anything but gave her a sharp look. What will happen to us if we pick some now? Javier asked. The devil will come with a big bag and take you away in it, he replied. Oh! we exclaimed. I had never seen the devil but I got scared. I have to go now, he continued, but remember, do not eat oranges from this tree or you will go to hell! And he left.

Javier, Octavio and I looked at Antonia, disappointed. She went to the tree, picked several oranges, peeled one and started to eat it. These are for you, she calmly said. But Antonia, what if the devil comes?! I asked her. We will give him some oranges, he will eat them and leave, she said smiling. I am a little scared, Javier said while peeling one. Antonia calmed us, eat these oranges because they are healthy and they will erase your fears and give you joy. That was exactly what happened. Javier and I felt so good that we said, let's call all our friends! Let's call everybody, Antonia added, the whole town should be happy and there are plenty of oranges here! Early that evening, a lot of people gathered around the tree and ate oranges. I had indigestion and now I feel better, a woman said. I was sad and I am not anymore, another one added. The parish priest came back late when everyone was gone. He looked at the tree. It is still very full, he thought aloud, those children haven't taken any oranges, and he went inside his home. The following days and for several weeks, whenever the parish priest wasn't around (he had to say masses, and perform baptisms, weddings, and other stuff in small neighboring towns that had churches but no priests), the children, and adults, too, went to pick and eat oranges from the moonlight orange tree, as we called it.

The moonlight orange tree gave us thousands of oranges the following season, too. And the following and the following. In the end, the parish priest realized that people were taking oranges from the tree. He had even gone and asked don Ernesto, who owned a produce and fruit store, whether people were buying oranges or not. Don Ernesto had told him he wasn't selling many oranges anymore because it seemed people preferred tangerines now. I don't know why, however, the parish priest never threatened us with the devil again. Perhaps he finally understood he couldn't eat so many oranges by himself. Or perhaps, the oranges were making him a better person. One afternoon, he saw Javier and I climbing the tree and he told us, children, don't forget to take some for your parents! He sounded very sweet, just like the oranges. We said, thank you, sir, you are very generous and filled our arms to the brim.

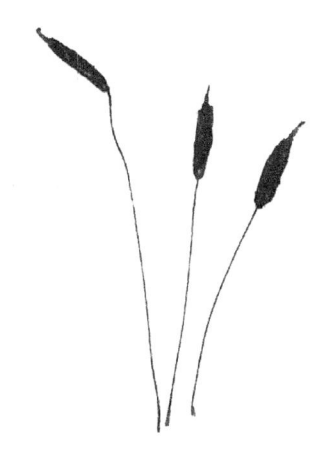

Cecilia

And there came Cecilia pushing a wheelbarrow. She was one of the oldest inhabitants of our town. People believed she was now around 117 years old… but who knows how old she was! Two years more, three years less, nobody knew her age. What everyone knew for sure was that she was immortal. She had talked about surviving horrendous storms and ferocious monsters. She said she had also survived three wars and that had been difficult.

She came pushing a wheelbarrow and stopped at the plaza. Honey, honey, for everyone! she shouted. A lot of people went to see what she had: a wheelbarrow loaded with jars of honey. I have decided this town needs honey, she told them, so here it is, take some jars for you and your neighbors. How did you get it? a man asked her. On the outskirts, to the east, that's where the bees and I work, we work together. The parish priest came forward and asked her, is this honey going to make people immortal, like you are? I never heard of any kind of honey that makes people immortal, she answered.

The parish priest wasn't happy with Cecilia. Well, he wasn't happy with many people, I should say, but I am now talking about Cecilia. The problem seemed to be her immortality. According to the church, the parish priest explained, it was a mortal sin for a mortal to be immortal. She was going to go to hell, for her sin. And here was another complication: she couldn't go to hell because she was immortal. Cecilia and the priest had had many discussions, arguments sometimes, because of this. She said she wasn't resisting death or even the rules of the church, but there was nothing she could do because she had been born like that. The parish priest once suggested she take herself to a natural or a man-produced calamity, like a shipwreck, a flood, another war, a volcanic blast, something like that. If you tried, you could die, he told her. Cecilia reminded him that to try on purpose to die in any of those calamities was like trying to commit suicide and the church didn't approve of suicide. In fact, she had once heard him saying that it was a mortal sin. The priest didn't insist: he did not want to go to hell for his suggestion.

Now at the plaza Cecilia assured the priest and everyone else that honey was a vital source of health but it didn't make anybody immortal. The parish priest left, without a jar. Next came a policeman. Do you have a permit to sell this in a public space? he asked her. I am not selling anything, she replied, I am giving this away to keep you healthy. But you are blocking the traffic, he insisted. What traffic? she asked. He sighed and left.

It was in this simple, direct way that Cecilia became the provider of honey for the town. Each week she came to the plaza pushing her wheelbarrow, and shouted, "Honey, honey, for everyone!" People enjoyed getting honey and getting honey for free was particularly enjoyable. We got used to this weekly honey giveaway. Just as we had gotten used to the stars coming closer, the birds singing in official ceremonies and Antonia talking with the moon. We decided this flood of honey was good for us and we took it in. As for Cecilia's immortality, it wasn't our concern. If it bothered the priest, it didn't bother us. After all, her immortality was the assurance that our town would forever have honey.

The Beginning

This happened
Long before my grandma arrived in town.
Long before Matilde was born with Pepe and María's help.
Long before the people, who would later exclaim oooooooooooooooooh
when Emilia smoked a pipe on one foot in the church's tower,
arrived in town.

Long before I was born.
Long before Carolina, who planted trees and organized the first bird's chorus,
arrived in town.
Long before horses and roosters were born.
Long before the parish priest, carrying a cross and saint Peter in a wheelbarrow,
arrived in town.
Long before my friends and Octavio, Javier's dog, were born.
Long before Esther and her husband, who came from very far away with five photographs, arrived in town.
Long before Aurora was born.
Long before the director of the post office, who later opened an office
and delivered letters, arrived in town.

This is what happened:
Somebody appeared on the horizon.
She was tired and lonely, had walked a long way
with her few belongings.
She was uncertain where she was.
She asked aloud, is anybody here?
She received no answer.
She knelt, looked at the earth and repeated the question.
Again. No answer.
She sighed and said, nobody is here.
I will stop here.
I will start a town right here.

She lifted a heavy stone, walked a few steps and dropped it:
This will be the town's axis, she said,
and I will be the first inhabitant.
Then, she built her house.

In those times, people coming from across the ocean:
farmers and artisans,
carpenters and bricklayers,
teachers and healers,
were eagerly looking for towns to settle in.
They had crossed the ocean
fleeing poverty, fleeing wars, fleeing persecutions,
fleeing all sorts of man-made disasters.

In those times, people were eagerly looking for towns.
Can we stay here? they asked.
You can stay, she answered, and help me build the plaza
in the place where I put the stone.
In those times and for a long time,
a plaza was the beginning of a town,
its point of reference:
a town without a plaza was not a town,
a plaza was the beginning
and the end: if the plaza was taken out
the town ceased to exist.

People built the plaza,
built houses and chicken coops,
built a school and a big room for dances,

marked streets and roads
and called themselves the inhabitants of the new town.

Then animals arrived:
Hens and roosters for the chicken coops.
Birds for the few trees/pigeons for the school's roof.
Horses for the stables and cows for the meadows.
Dogs for barking/ cats for purring and flies for nothing.

(There wasn't a river yet,
so fish and ducks and frogs and toads
had to delay their coming to the new town.)

The inhabitants had a hard time
deciding on a name for the town.
Because they had a hard time,
the town didn't get a name.
It got several names.

Some referred to it as
Julia Bustinza
who was the founder.
Some suggested names of saints,
but couldn't agree on which one.
Some called it
Cattail
because of the abundance of cattails.
Others simply called it
Cat
because of the abundance of cats.

Still others said,
this is a new town,
let's create a new name,
let's call it Pueblo Nuevo.

In those times and for a long time,
Pueblo Nuevo was the name
of almost every new town.
- Where do you live?
- In Pueblo Nuevo
- Where are you going?
- To Pueblo Nuevo
- Where is the dance this evening?
- In Pueblo Nuevo
For a long time,
wherever they lived,
people said they lived in Pueblo Nuevo.
This had to be corrected, otherwise:
visitors went to the wrong town;
after pasturing, animals returned to the wrong stable;
grandparents went to the wrong town to visit their grandchildren;
and messengers spent days looking for the right Pueblo Nuevo
in order to deliver their messages.

My town then decided unanimously on
Cattail.

The inhabitants of Cattail
had a hard time

deciding which season was winter
which one was summer
and the others in between.
They had come from lands
where the seasons were fixed:
July was always summer,
December was always winter.
But in Pueblo Nuevo, later Cattail,
somebody had moved them around
and July was cold
and December was hot.
What are we going to do? some wondered.
We don't have to do anything, others replied.
Let's follow the seasons as they are here, all agreed.

Let's go to Pueblo Nuevo because it is new,
my grandma said when she and her husband were looking for a place
to settle.
Pueblo Nuevo is that way, her husband indicated, crossing the road.
No, Pueblo Nuevo is this way, to the left, she replied.
And they came to Pueblo Nuevo, later Cattail.
And they settled in.
I can stop wars from this place, she said after a while.
How do you know? her husband asked.
Her answer:
everybody, or almost everybody, hates wars here.
How do you know? her husband insisted.
I dreamed it…
and I dreamed it again.

I dreamed it! Eva, the storyteller, exclaimed,
people will listen to my stories in this town,
"there was once a whale who hated wars…"
Well, all whales hate wars!
"and she tried to eliminate all the weapons in the world,
the sea couldn't believe it and told her,
'take a break, go to a river for a while, rest my dear,
you will have time to do that later,' so she went to a river."
And this said, Eva settled in.
(But Eva, there wasn't a river yet in Cattail!)

Antonia came too,
she looked up at the night:
There is going to be a beautiful moon here,
and when it is full moon I will be able to touch it
with my hand,
and here she stayed.

Emilia arrived on a rainy day.
She was the only one who arrived
riding a vehicle: her bicycle with wings.
Emilia had been a travelling clown,
but she came here,
saw her sister here,
saw there wasn't any clown here,
and here she stayed.

Paula came with her mother.

Paula wanted a place to sing,
to sing openly and loudly.
I don't know why, maybe I dreamed it,
but I will be able to sing openly and loudly here,
she thought.
And here mother and daughter stayed.

Aurora came with doña Rosa.
Both in multi-colored dresses on a spring day,
loved the smell of jasmine and the elegance of wisteria,
looked at each other and agreed:
here we will stay.

Carolina, Javier and Octavio arrived
early on a rainy morning.
Carolina realized very soon that Cattail needed trees.
Trees, here and there, she thought, I will work in this town.

But then
some misguided mind said,
we need a government. Otherwise, chaos will reign.
We need a government, the newly arrived parish priest repeated,
and a church.

That year,
on a very stormy night,
in the month of July,
government and church were installed.

The misguided mind became the first mayor of the town.
He became the first disliked person.
He became wealthy.
He became sick.
He died.

But heaven and hell and their institutions
had been created
and they stayed.
As in most places on earth, they stayed.

However, however, however,
we had Antonia, Carolina, Eva, Matilde, Aurora,
Emilia, Victoria, Lisa, Paula, grandma…
And many others it would take me another book to mention!

And the town survived, resisted, prospered.
And the moon decided to be bigger and brighter
on quiet winter nights,
so Micha, the cat, would stare at the moon
and think, amazed, meow this town is unique!

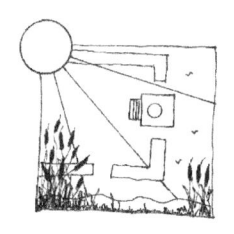

The End
(for now)

Matilde said,
"When he was younger, Mark Twain would remember anything, whether it had happened or not."

Aurora added,
"Remembering is sometimes like dreaming."

Printed in Great Britain
by Amazon